The Farmer's Promise

Written by Elaine Kiklis
Illustrated by Abby Sullivan

The Farmer's Promise is based on the wonders of childhood and magic.

Published in the United States by Riverhaven Books,
www.RiverhavenBooks.com

ISBN : 978-1-951854-16-4

Printed in the United States of America
by Country Press, Lakeville, Massachusetts

Designed and Edited by Stephanie Lynn Blackman
Whitman, MA

**To my grandson Logan,
Never stop believing in magic!**

Do you believe in magic?

Once upon a time,

a farmer named Logan lived in the town of Greenville. He worked hard to take care of all the animals on his farm. And after all of them were fed and had fresh bedding each day, he would sit alone on his favorite tree stump to rest.

As he watched the buzzing bees and dragonflies who flew about the wildflowers he would say, "Hello, little friends."

Then he would sigh and say, "I wish you could talk back to me."

Farmer Logan didn't know that a dragonfly from the kingdom of Magic was watching him each day.

The dragonfly hid in the flowers and listened. And the more he learned, the more he knew he had to do something to grant the farmer's wish.

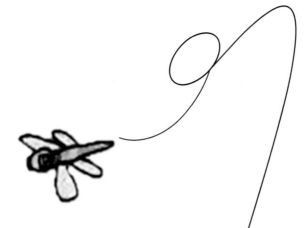

The dragonfly returned to the kingdom of Magic and told the rulers of the kingdom about the farmer and the kindness he showed to all of his animals.

They all agreed that Farmer Logan deserved to have his wish granted.

The next morning as the farmer walked from the big red barn to his tree stump, magic was about to happen. Magic that came with a promise!

On that morning, a beautifully colored dragonfly landed on the farmer's shoulder and did not fly away. Farmer Logan looked at him and said, "Well, hello, colorful dragonfly. What can I do for you today?"

To Farmer Logan's surprise, the dragonfly answered him!

"I am here to grant your wish, Farmer Logan, and to bring a little magic to your farm."

"What type of magic?"

"Magic that only lasts if you can keep a promise," the dragonfly told him. "How would you like it if when your animals talk, you could understand them?"

Farmer Logan said, "I'd love to be able to know what they're saying. What do I need to promise?"

"You must promise to not tell anyone about the wish you've been granted."

"Can I tell my animals?" Farmer Logan asked.

The dragonfly smiled. "You can. But only because they are your closest friends, and you should never keep important secrets from those you love."

Farmer Logan was so excited that he jumped up and down five times. "Oh, what a wonderful gift that would be. Thank you so much!"

Farmer Logan was very happy as he headed back to the barn.

Shirley, a large black and white sheepdog, greeted him at the door. "Hello, Farmer Logan. Do you have a special job for me today?"

Farmer Logan was so excited to understand his friends. He smiled and said, "Yes, Shirley. Can you please help me gather all of the sheep? It is shearing day, and they need to have their winter wool coats removed so they won't be too hot."

"I'll round up all of the sheep and put them into the pen. That will make it easier for you, Farmer Logan."

"Thank you, Shirley."

When Farmer Logan went to the pen, he saw how hot some of the sheep were. As he was counting them, he saw that Shirley was worried about something and asked, "What is it, Shirley? What's wrong?"

Shirley paced back and forth a bit as she told him, "I gathered all of the sheep I could find, but Sadie is missing. She wasn't with the others, and none of them know where she could be."

Farmer Logan was worried.

"Shirley, you know the sheep very well. Is there any other place where Sadie may have gone?"

Shirley thought very hard. "Well, she isn't supposed to go there alone, but it is possible that she is high on the hill behind the barn where there's a field of white clover."

"Let's go look," he said.

The farmer and Shirley reached the top of the hill and saw Sadie standing in the middle of the sweet white clover, munching away.

Sadie knew she was in trouble. "I'm sorry, Farmer Logan. I just love this clover so much that I can't stop eating it."

"I was very worried when we couldn't find you, Sadie."

"And I was worried too," said Shirley.

Sadie stopped eating and said, "I'm sorry." And she really was.

As the three walked, he told Sadie that it was to be shearing day for all of the sheep. But Sadie's belly was so full of clover, the farmer knew he would not be able to able to shear her wool until tomorrow.

Sadie tried not to smile, but she loved her wooly coat and was glad to have it for one more day.

When the three of them arrived back to the barnyard, the chickens and ducks were making a lot of noise. They were squabbling over a single ear of corn.

Farmer Logan walked towards Mabel the duck and Penny the chicken, picked up the ear of corn from the ground, and asked, "Why are you both so upset?"

"The chickens eat almost all of the food," Mabel said. "There are only ten ducks, but there are twenty chickens, and they aren't very good about sharing."

Penny could see that Mabel was right. "Farmer Logan, from now on, can you feed the chickens in the barnyard and the ducks in the meadow?"

"That's a wonderful idea!" Mabel said. "Can we do that, Farmer Logan?"

"Absolutely," he said. The farmer was so glad he could speak to his animals and that everyone would be happy and work together.

Boris and Clyde, the two plow horses, galloped up to the barn.

"Can we be of help today, Farmer Logan?" Boris asked.

"Yes, you can. We need to plow the field. It is time to plant the corn and carrots."

"We're ready," Clyde said.

"Oh, can I help?" asked Olive the donkey.

Farmer Logan said, "Of course!" and laughed as she ran alongside the plow.

**Olive always thought of herself
as a big plow horse too.**

After the field was finished, Farmer Logan went to check on the goats and pigs. Sometimes they found ways to sneak under the fence to where the crops were planted, but the kindly farmer would never be angry. He would shoo them away.

Today he said, "We need to wait until all of the plants grow bigger and then we will have a wonderful garden of food."

The next day as the farmer walked into the big red barn, he called to his favorite cow. "Come, Daisy, it's time for milking."

"Coming, Farmer Logan," she answered.

This made him smile.

"Farmer Logan, do you think we can go to the pond after milking today?" Daisy asked.

The farmer said yes and thought how very lucky he was to have friends to talk to at last.

When the milking was almost finished, Felix the cat walked into the barn. Felix always came at the end of milking, and Farmer Logan always gave him a bowl of fresh milk.

"You spoil him," Annabel, the oldest cow, said. Annabel did not like sharing her milk with Felix.

The farmer just smiled in his kindly way and put the bowl of milk down for Felix. "It is very important to share, Annabel, and Felix loves your milk."

"I'm sorry, Felix," Annabel said. "Farmer Logan is right. I am happy to share my milk with you."

Felix looked at her and said, "Thank you, Annabel. I do love your milk!"

Life on the farm was peaceful and happy in all the years that followed. Farmer Logan was forever grateful for the gift he had been given so long ago, and he never broke his promise to the magic dragonfly.

Winking one of his big green eyes, the dragonfly from the kingdom of Magic said, "It's easy to make a promise, but it's magical to keep one!"